D0719006

The Selfish Giant

Oscar Wilde

Illustrated and abridged *by*

Alexis Deacon

HUTCHINSON

To Gladys, my grandmother,
who is neither selfish nor giant.
A. D.

Some other books written and illustrated
by Alexis Deacon

Slow Loris
Beegu
While You Are Sleeping
Croc and Bird

THE SELFISH GIANT
A HUTCHINSON BOOK 978 0091 89364 4

Published in Great Britain by Hutchinson,
an imprint of Random House Children's Publishers UK
A Random House Group Company

This edition published 2013

1 3 5 7 9 10 8 6 4 2

Abridgement copyright © Alexis Deacon, 2013
Illustrations copyright © Alexis Deacon, 2013

The right of Alexis Deacon to be identified as the abridger and illustrator
of this work has been asserted in accordance with the Copyright, Designs and Patents Act 1988.

All rights reserved. No part of this publication may be reproduced, stored in a retrieval system,
or transmitted in any form or by any means, electronic, mechanical, photocopying, recording or otherwise,
without the prior permission of the publishers.

RANDOM HOUSE CHILDREN'S PUBLISHERS UK
61−63 Uxbridge Road, London W5 5SA

www.**randomhousechildrens**.co.uk
www.**randomhouse**.co.uk

Addresses for companies within The Random House Group Limited can be found at:
www.randomhouse.co.uk/offices.htm

THE RANDOM HOUSE GROUP Limited Reg. No. 954009

A CIP catalogue record for this book is available from the British Library.

Printed in China

The Random House Group Limited supports the Forest Stewardship Council® (FSC®), the leading international
forest-certification organisation. Our books carrying the FSC label are printed on FSC®-certified paper.
FSC is the only forest certification scheme supported by the leading environmental organisations,
including Greenpeace. Our paper procurement policy can be found at
www.randomhouse.co.uk/environment.

EVERY AFTERNOON, as they were coming from school,
the children used to go and play in the Giant's garden.

It was a large, lovely garden, with soft green grass.
Here and there over the grass stood beautiful flowers
like stars, and there were twelve peach-trees that in
the Springtime broke out into delicate blossoms of pink
and pearl, and in the Autumn bore rich fruit. The birds
sat on the trees and sang so sweetly that the children used
to stop their games in order to listen to them.

One day the Giant came back.

"What are you doing here?"

he cried in a very gruff voice, and the children ran away.

"My own garden is my own garden," said the Giant; "anyone can understand that, and I will allow nobody to play in it but myself."

So he built a high wall all round it, and put up a notice board.

He was a very selfish giant.

Spring came, and all over the country
there were little blossoms and little birds.
Only in the garden of the Selfish Giant
it was still Winter. The birds did not care
to sing in it, as there were no children,
and the trees forgot to blossom.

The only people who were pleased were the Snow and the Frost. "Spring has forgotten this garden," they cried, "so we will live here all the year round."

The Snow covered up the grass and the Frost painted all the trees silver. Then they invited the North Wind to stay with them . . .

. . . and he came.

    He roared all day about the garden
and blew the chimney-pots down.
"This is a delightful spot," he said;
"we must ask the Hail on a visit."

So the Hail came.

TRES
WILL
BE
PROSF

"I cannot understand why the Spring
is so late in coming," said the Selfish Giant,
as he sat and looked out at his cold white garden;
"I hope there will be a change in the weather."
But the Spring never came, nor the Summer.
The Autumn gave golden fruit to every garden, but to
the Giant's garden she gave none. "He is too selfish," she said.
So it was always Winter there, and the North Wind, and the Hail,
and the Frost, and the Snow danced about through the trees.

One morning the Giant was lying awake in bed when he heard some lovely music. It was really only a little linnet singing outside his window, but it was so long since he had heard a bird sing in his garden that it seemed to him to be the most beautiful music in the world. Then the Hail stopped dancing over his head, and the North Wind ceased roaring, and a delicious perfume came to him through the open casement.

"I believe Spring has come at last," said the Giant; and he jumped out of bed and looked out.

What did he see?

He saw a most wonderful sight.

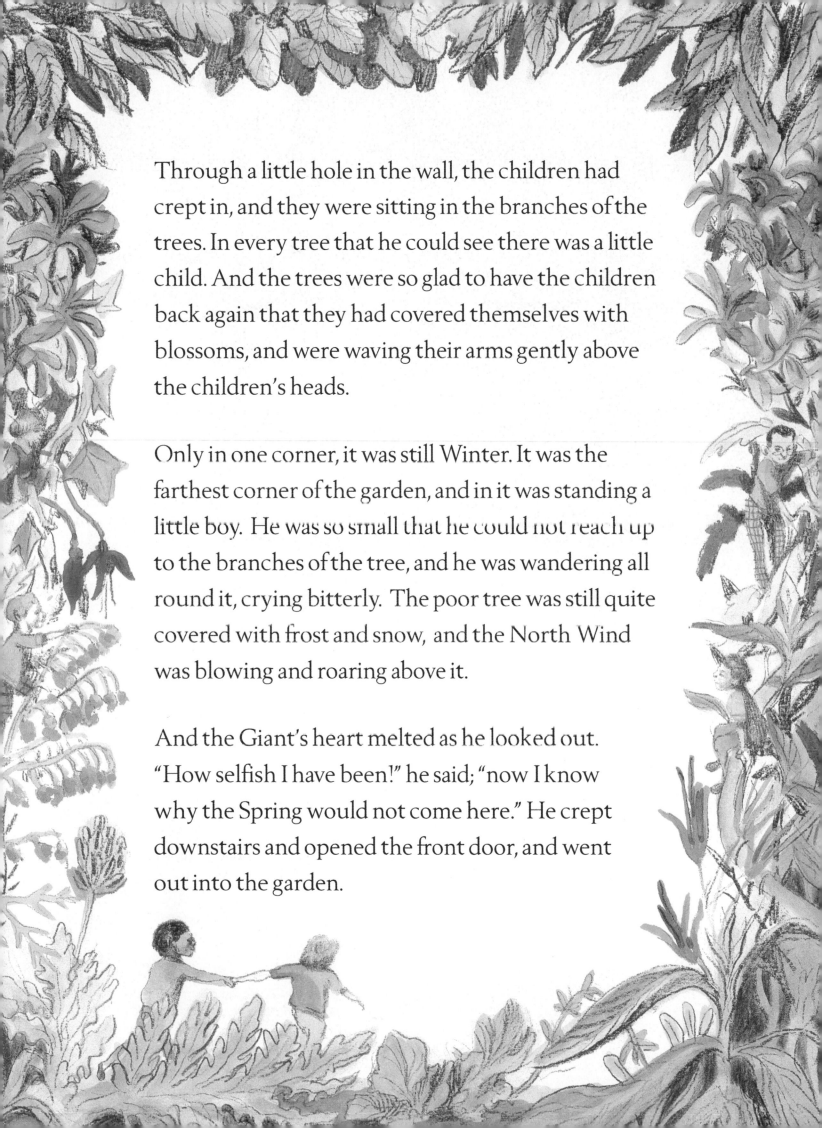

Through a little hole in the wall, the children had crept in, and they were sitting in the branches of the trees. In every tree that he could see there was a little child. And the trees were so glad to have the children back again that they had covered themselves with blossoms, and were waving their arms gently above the children's heads.

Only in one corner, it was still Winter. It was the farthest corner of the garden, and in it was standing a little boy. He was so small that he could not reach up to the branches of the tree, and he was wandering all round it, crying bitterly. The poor tree was still quite covered with frost and snow, and the North Wind was blowing and roaring above it.

And the Giant's heart melted as he looked out. "How selfish I have been!" he said; "now I know why the Spring would not come here." He crept downstairs and opened the front door, and went out into the garden.

But when the children saw him they were so
frightened that they all ran away, and the garden
became Winter again. Only the little boy did not run,
for his eyes were so full of tears that he did not see
the Giant coming.

And the Giant stole up behind him and took him gently in his hand, and put him up into the tree. And the tree broke at once into blossom, and the birds came and sang on it, and the little boy stretched out his two arms and flung them round the Giant's neck, and kissed him.

And the other children, when they saw that the Giant was not wicked any longer, came running back, and with them came the Spring.

"It is your garden now, little children," said the Giant,
and he took a great axe and knocked down the wall.

And when the people were going to market at twelve
o'clock they found the Giant playing with the children . . .

. . . in the most beautiful garden they had ever seen.